MY READING NEIGHBORHOOD
Kindergarten Sight Word Stories

Sam Is Six

Sara E. Hoffmann

illustrated by Shelley Dieterichs

D1551021

Consultant:

Marla Conn, MS, Education
Reading/Literacy Specialist

LernerClassroom™

MINNEAPOLIS

I am Sam.

I live on First Street.

Today I turn six!

I open my presents.

I play a game.

I blow out my candles.

Then I eat cake!